The Paper House

The Paper House

LOIS PETERSON

ORCA BOOK PUBLISHERS

Library and Archives Canada Cataloguing in Publication

Peterson, Lois J., 1952-
The paper house / Lois Peterson.
(Orca young readers)

Issued also in electronic formats.
ISBN 978-1-4598-0051-9

I. Title. II. Series: Orca young readers
PS8631.E832P36 2012   JC813'.6   C2011-907767-1

First published in the United States, 2012
Library of Congress Control Number: 2011943725

Summary: A mural on a tin shack brings hope and happiness
to a girl in the slums of Nairobi.

MIX
Paper from
responsible sources
FSC
www.fsc.org   FSC® C004071

Orca Book Publishers is dedicated to preserving the environment and has printed this book on paper certified by the Forest Stewardship Council®.

Orca Book Publishers gratefully acknowledges the support for its publishing programs provided by the following agencies: the Government of Canada through the Canada Book Fund and the Canada Council for the Arts, and the Province of British Columbia through the BC Arts Council and the Book Publishing Tax Credit.

Cover artwork by Scott Plumbe

ORCA BOOK PUBLISHERS
PO Box 5626, Stn. B
Victoria, BC Canada
V8R 6S4

ORCA BOOK PUBLISHERS
PO Box 468
Custer, WA USA
98240-0468

www.orcabook.com
Printed and bound in Canada.

15 14 13 12   •   4 3 2 1

For Shelley and Mohammed,
and their nephews Harrison and Isaiah.

Chapter One

Safiyah stood ankle-deep in garbage near the top of the dump. Below her lay the Kibera slum, a patchwork of rusty tin roofs. A thick blanket of cloud and dirty smoke hid the concrete buildings and busy roads of nearby Nairobi.

Not far from where Safiyah stood, a pack of small boys tussled like mangy dogs over a heap of old clothes. Suddenly, one broke away and leaped at her. "What have you got there?" he yelled.

She held the old magazines high in the air where he couldn't reach them. "You can't have them."

The other boys were watching.

"Let me see." With each jump, the boy's hands came a little closer. "Hey, you lot!" he yelled. "See what she's got."

"It's just paper." Safiyah could hear her voice shaking. She had seen gangs of boys corner lone girls before. Sometimes they beat them up or stole things from them. But the boy's friends had already found something more interesting in the garbage.

When she hid the handful of magazines behind her back, the boy leaped at her again. "Let me see the pictures."

Safiyah sold most of the stuff she found at the dump. It was the only way to make money for a pound of maize or some tea. Sometimes a breadfruit for Cucu, her grandmother, who loved them so much.

People would buy almost anything she dug up: old clothes, cracked dishes, tins and old tires. Once Safiyah found an old clock that still worked, and they had eaten well for a week.

Today she was looking for paper to fill the cracks in the wood and metal walls of their house. Maybe Cucu would get well if Safiyah could keep out the smoke and the cold night air. Then Cucu could take care of the house and make the meals so that Safiyah could go to school like her best friend, Pendo.

But for that you needed more money than Safiyah could make selling stuff from the dump.

"I want to see," screeched the little boy as he grabbed at her again.

Safiyah slipped and slithered away from his grasping hands. She waded through plastic cartons and torn packaging. Bottles and jagged cans tumbled down all around her. Clumps of plastic bags squelched under her feet. Ripped newspaper and stinky diapers clung to her legs.

Another landslide of smelly garbage fell around the little boy as he scrambled down behind her. "Let me see." He yanked her arm.

Safiyah twisted away. But the boy squeezed his thin arms around her waist. He was hurting her, but she wasn't going to cry.

"It's just old magazines." She held the papers out of reach.

"I want to look at the cars," whined the boy. "There are always pictures of cars."

"I need them." As Safiyah pulled away, she almost fell back onto the garbage. Dense swarms of flies rose into the air. The sickly stench was worse now.

She was getting used to filthy puddles of water everywhere and the smell of burning garbage and rotten food. But the stink was always worse at the garbage dump.

The boy lunged at her again. He pulled one of her pigtails.

She slapped him.

He yanked her so hard that they both fell back into the shifting garbage. Something sharp poked Safiyah's back. A wad of slimy stuff clung to her leg.

The smell got worse as Safiyah and the little boy tussled.

Suddenly, the boy's weight lifted off her. "What's this then?" Deep scars ran down the cheeks of a tall teenager who held the smaller boy by one arm.

His tightly curled hair was dyed red. Blade! The gang leader was everywhere you looked in Kibera.

Cucu was always warning Safiyah to stay clear of the gangs that roamed the slum. They stole cell phones and radios and cut people with knives. Mr. Zuma's bicycle shop had once been held up by a gang with guns and sticks. Safiyah had sometimes seen Blade lounging against walls, flicking his knife open and closed, open and closed, or swaggering through the streets with his tough friends, sending people scattering.

"Run away home, little girl," Blade told her now, "before I let this brat loose on you." His eyes were big and shiny. "Your *cucu* will be waiting for you."

"I'm not a little girl," she told him, even though some people said she was small for ten. How did he know about her grandmother? Safiyah wondered.

"Go on!" Blade held tight to the little boy, who was trying to squirm away. "Get out of here," he ordered. "I'll take care of this brat."

Safiyah didn't wait to be told again. She ran along the alley, leaping across heaps of garbage and puddles of smelly water. She jumped over babies playing in the dirt. She darted around women gossiping between the densely packed shacks.

Cucu had told her that gangs recruited boys when they were young. And if they didn't want to join, they were beaten until they did. What would Blade do with the little boy? she wondered as she raced home.

Safiyah kept running without looking back. She had no time to worry about a boy she did not know, or to wonder why a gang leader would want to help her.

Chapter Two

When Safiyah reached her own street at last, she slowed down and tried to stop panting. Cucu would want to know why she was out of breath. She didn't like it when Safiyah was away from home too long. And Safiyah knew that her grandmother would give her a talking to if she found out she had been in a fight.

A huddle of school kids came out of an alley between the shacks. They all wore red sweaters and blue shorts or skirts. Her friend Pendo broke away from the others and ran to catch up with Safiyah. She wrinkled her nose as she looked her up and down. "You stink, Saffy."

"I had a fight with a boy at the dump."

"Oh." Pendo shrugged. "I only got nine out of ten on my spelling." She was not interested in fights at the dump. Kids—and sometimes adults—were always fighting over the garbage, most of which came from Nairobi.

"Nine out of ten is good," Safiyah told her. "Maybe you will get them all right next time." The two girls linked arms and walked on together.

Safiyah was filled with relief when she saw Cucu asleep on her bench outside their shack. She always worried when she left her grandmother alone to run errands in the neighborhood. She dreaded coming home to find her dead, the way she had found her mother soon after they had come to Kibera. Safiyah had been washing their clothes in the nearby ditch when her mother died. They had come here for her mother to find work after the crops failed and there was no food in the village.

Now Cucu was all the family Safiyah had. She could never survive alone in this awful place if something happened to her grandmother.

Cucu's skin was ashen as she dozed against the wall. Sweat ran down her cheeks. She opened her eyes as Pendo and Safiyah hurried to her side. "My lovely girls." She smiled.

"Can Pendo stay and play?" asked Safiyah.

"Go home and change first," Cucu told Pendo. "Your mother would not want you to dirty your lovely uniform."

"I've got chores," said Pendo. "But I will see you later, Saffy." As Pendo darted away, her schoolbag banged against her hip and her skirt whipped against her legs

"Obedient child," said Cucu as Pendo dashed along the alley. The red of her sweater flickered in the distance like flame from a fire.

Safiyah put her magazines on Cucu's lap. "Look."

"Something for me?" asked her grandmother. "Me and my old eyes." She glanced at a bright cover of a woman wearing a yellow dress.

"They are for patching the walls," said Safiyah. "But you can look at them first."

Cucu stroked Safiyah's face. "What would I do without you?" She coughed harshly into a bunched rag.

Safiyah ran indoors and fetched a bowl. She held it for her grandmother to spit in until the coughing stopped. She stroked her cucu's shoulder as she slumped back against the wall with her eyes closed.

When she was sure the coughing fit was over, Safiyah ran across the alley to empty the bowl.

Little flecks of blood floated on the surface. This was the second time Safiyah had seen blood after one of Cucu's coughing fits.

Safiyah wiped the bowl with her sleeve. If she told anyone, her grandmother might have to go to the hospital. Some people who ended up there never came home again.

Chapter Three

That evening, Safiyah turned the pages of the magazines she had found at the dump while her grandmother watched from under their thin blankets.

Cucu couldn't read. Nor could Safiyah. She had not been to school since they left their village, two day's bus ride away. School lessons were often free here in Kibera, thanks to rich people who donated money. But a student's family was responsible for their uniform and books, which cost money—money Safiyah and her grandmother would never have.

"Lovely shoes," said Cucu. In the picture Safiyah held out to her, a man leaned back in his chair smoking a cigarette. His shoes, with little tassels in the middle, shone like polished wood.

Cucu always wore a pair of old runners with holes cut away for her bunions. Safiyah sometimes wore a cracked pair of flip-flops. But she went barefoot most of the time.

Safiyah liked the pictures of ladies' clothes and fancy houses. And the ones of models with smooth makeup. But when she pressed her face against a picture of a bottle of perfume all she could smell was the stink of garbage.

The little boy at the dump was right. There were lots of pictures of cars. A green one with an open roof and a red one with silver in the middle of the wheels. There was even a row of white cars with pretty girls sitting on them, their yellow hair streaming behind.

In Safiyah's village, one man drove a noisy truck he had built himself. Here, she sometimes played in the skeletons of old cars abandoned beside the railroad tracks. She had never been in a car that worked.

Safiyah tore out the pictures she liked best. She put them in a pile. "I'm going to keep some to put on the walls after I fill all the cracks," she told her grandmother. "But how can I make them stay?"

"Some maize flour and a little water will make a paste," said Cucu as she fanned through a handful of pictures. She held them close to her face to study them in the dim light of the shack.

"We don't have flour." Safiyah gathered all the pages that were just a gray muddle of writing. "But maybe this will work." She tore the paper into small pieces, dipped each one in the bucket of water that was kept under the bed, and then twisted each scrap into a little roll.

Cucu watched as Safiyah climbed on the bed to stuff paper into the cracks in the walls. Safiyah moved their little stove and a basket of old clothes out of the way to reach into the corners. Cucu pointed out where to put the scraps of paper, guided by the light that showed through the gaps.

Later, when her grandmother fell asleep, Safiyah sat on the end of the bed listening to her wheezy breath. There were still lots more gaps in the walls, but if she used up all the magazines she'd found at the dump, she would no longer be able to look at the pictures of fancy clothes, nice houses and food.

"What are you doing?" Pendo stood in the doorway in her striped shorts and a green sweater with a hole in the elbow. She was barefoot now too.

"Shhh." Safiyah gestured to her sleeping grandmother and led Pendo outside.

Pendo took a picture from Safiyah's hand. "Look at all that blue water." A glinting swimming pool was shaped like a big apple. "My uncle went to the ocean once," she boasted. "The water stretches out forever, he said. Just like this."

"These are the best pictures. I stuffed the others in the walls to fill the cracks," Safiyah said. "If I can keep out the cold and smoke, maybe Cucu will get better."

She wanted to tell Pendo how afraid she was that her grandmother might die. But the words were too hard to say aloud. Even to her best friend.

The girls peeked through the doorway at Cucu. The light from the flickering lamp made the hollows in her cheeks look deeper. All the sadness of their hard life showed in Cucu's face, thought Safiyah.

What did her own sleeping face look like? she wondered. Especially when she had nightmares all night. She wanted to tell Pendo about the blood she'd seen in the bowl earlier. But Pendo would tell a grownup, and Cucu would end up in hospital.

And then what will happen to me? thought Safiyah. She swallowed hard. "Let's look at the other pictures," she said. She blew out the lamp and tightened the thin blanket around Cucu's shoulder. She pulled the frayed curtain across the doorway and went outside again, so they wouldn't wake her grandmother.

Chapter Four

While Cucu slept indoors, the two girls spread the pictures on the ground close to the house, out of the way of passing feet and bicycles.

Evening was a busy time in Kibera. The streets filled up with people coming home from jobs as maids or drivers or from tending their market stalls. They gathered to discuss the day's news. They strolled along arm-in-arm in laughing groups or ducked into the tea shop to visit with friends.

Back in Safiyah's village, everyone had gathered in the shade after a long day of work. Babies who had spent the day tucked into their mothers' shawls played in the dry earth. Women cooked the evening meal under the branches of the plane trees. And every night Safiyah fell asleep to the comforting sounds of village life.

There, Safiyah had been surrounded by family and villagers. People she had known all her life. Here, there was just her and Cucu, with strangers—some of them dangerous and frightening—everywhere.

Everything was so different in Kibera. The noises were louder and the smells stronger. Flies hovered above trenches of mucky water. Garbage lay everywhere. Packs of dogs roamed the alleys, barking and howling, rooting for food and getting in snarling fights. Flocks of birds scavenged through the garbage dump and sat in noisy rows on the power lines above the railroad tracks. Fires sometimes destroyed whole rows of shacks. Gangs threatened old people and women and little kids.

Safiyah was often woken in the middle of the night by shouting, crying and terrible screams. "Go to sleep," Cucu would say as she stroked her back. "It's none of our business." But still Safiyah lay wide awake for hours, weeping quietly into her blankets as she remembered how safe she had felt back in their village, when her mother was still alive.

"These would look good on the walls," said Pendo as she flipped through the pile of pictures. She sat on

Cucu's bench, swinging her legs. "My mother only lets us put up pictures of Jesus."

Pendo's family attended the church that met every Sunday morning in a warehouse near the railroad tracks. Sometimes Safiyah stood in the back and sang along with the hymns. But she always ran home as soon as the collection bowl was passed around.

It was too far for Cucu to walk. Instead, she stayed on her bench and listened to the hymns drifting down the lanes.

As Safiyah watched Pendo leafing through the colored papers, pictures started to form in her head. The bright patterns of the ladies' hats and shawls and the glowing red robes of the choir when everyone crammed into church on Sundays. In her mind she saw the glorious mix of shapes and colors that changed the dark and smelly warehouse church into a garden full of light.

Even if it was just for one day a week.

Safiyah stepped into the lane to look back at her shack. "I'm going to put these pictures on the walls," she told Pendo

"That was my idea!"

"I'm going to put them outside," Safiyah said. "So everyone can see."

Pendo stood beside Safiyah and studied the shack. "How?"

"I need scissors," Safiyah told her. "To cut out the best pictures. Can you get some from school?"

"Maybe," said Pendo.

"Can you get paste too?"

"We have big jars of it." As Pendo nodded, her tiny braids danced up and down. "Mr. Littlejohn will give me some if I tell him it is for an art project. He says everyone needs to be creative." She held up the picture of the swimming pool. "Can I keep this one?" She folded it up and put it in her pocket before Safiyah could answer. "Where did you get all the pictures anyway?" she asked.

"From the dump," Safiyah told her. "Guess who was there?"

"Who?" asked Pendo.

"Blade. That big boy with the yellow pants and the marks down his face."

Pendo frowned. "He and his gang strut around like they are the bosses of Kibera." She shuddered. "You better stay away from him."

"He broke up the fight between me and another kid."

"Did he hurt you?" asked Pendo.

"He told me to go home," Safiyah told her. "He knows about Cucu."

"How do you know?"

"He told me to hurry home to her," Safiyah said.

Pendo shrugged. "That was just a good guess. Lots of kids live with their grandmothers." She folded another picture and stuffed it her pocket. "Don't go near him again, Saffy. I've heard awful things about his gang."

The alley was filling with shadows. Smoke from the neighbors' supper fires drifted between the shacks. Through some doorways, Safiyah could see people eating their meals in pools of flickering light. Others shared a cot while they played cards or mancala.

Soon after they had arrived, Mr. Zuma had told Cucu and Safiyah that about half a million people lived in Kibera. Even though her own neighborhood was crammed with people, half a million was more than she could imagine in one place!

"I have to go," Pendo said. She handed the stack of pictures back to Safiyah. "See you tomorrow."

"Don't forget to ask about the scissors and paste," Safiyah told her.

"I won't."

Safiyah watched her friend trot home. How nice it must be to go home to a warm house where your parents and brother waited for you, perhaps with a nice supper, steaming hot, smelling lovely. Neither she nor Cucu had eaten since morning. But there was only enough soup for one meal. They would share it for tomorrow's breakfast.

Safiyah took her pictures indoors where Cucu coughed in her sleep. She dipped her cup into their water bucket. As she drank, making a face at the smell, she imagined colorful pictures covering the outside of her house. And how warm and cozy it would be inside, once all the cracks in the walls were filled.

Chapter Five

Safiyah was kept awake much of the night by Cucu's cough. Next morning she was groggy and thick-headed.

She took her pictures outside and sat on Cucu's bench. She watched Mr. Lukomo push his barrow of old clothes toward the market. Mrs. Simon herded her three small children along, with a huge bundle of washing balanced on her head. A man with a broken bicycle slung across his back hurried past, his sandals flapping. A row of birds chattered on the power lines above the railroad tracks.

Safiyah wanted to remind Pendo to ask Mr. Littlejohn for scissors and paste. But when schoolchildren with bulging backpacks passed in a noisy huddle, Pendo was not among them.

Pendo had told her that her teacher lived on the Nairobi side of the railroad tracks. He had come to Kenya to help set up Pendo's school, which had been started with money from other countries. At first none of the teachers were African. Then all the Americans went home except Mr. Littlejohn.

Pendo boasted about the motorcycle he drove into the countryside on the weekends. She described his smart clothes and made Safiyah giggle by imitating his drawly American accent.

Pendo said that one day she might marry Mr. Littlejohn.

He was so pasty and white, he reminded Safiyah of a bowl of porridge. She planned to marry a smart African man who wore a shiny gray suit and drove a big car. One who lived in a mansion behind gates that someone opened and closed for him. Or perhaps she would marry a tall tribal leader with scars on his cheeks and the proud bearing of a warrior.

She found herself thinking about the boy called Blade. Maybe he was dangerous. But he was as tall as a warrior and very beautiful in his yellow pants, pulled high above his waist with a thick belt.

"What are you going to do with those?"

Startled, Safiyah stood up. "What do you want?" She had just been thinking about him and here he was!

"Don't you remember me?" Blade asked.

She held her pictures behind her back.

He stepped toward her.

A shriek escaped Safiyah's mouth.

"Saffy?" Cucu hobbled out, leaning on her stick. She grabbed Safiyah's arm and pulled her tightly against her side. "What are you doing here?" she asked Blade.

"Good morning, grandmother." He smiled and bowed.

"Don't you grandmother me," said Cucu. "I know who you are. And I know you're up to no good."

He shrugged. "I was just passing. I met your granddaughter yesterday."

Cucu turned on Safiyah. "Where did you meet this boy?" she asked.

"At the water vendor's," Safiyah lied. If she admitted she had met him at the dump, he might mention the fight with the little boy.

He winked at Safiyah over Cucu's head. "There was a long lineup."

Safiyah avoided looking at her grandmother, who prodded the boy's chest with her stick. "I know all about you," she told him.

"I doubt it." He narrowed his eyes.

"How dare you speak back to me!" Cucu screeched. "Do you know how old I am, to be spoken to like that!"

"As old as the hills, Granny. And the waters of the Gulf of Guinea that lap our shores. As old as the sky that keeps watch over us…"

"Cheeky boy!" Cucu looked flustered. She flapped one hand in the air. "Get out of here." She rapped his arm with her stick.

Blade stuck his hands in his pockets. He bowed lightly to Cucu, then to Safiyah. "You need more pictures?" he said. "You tell me, and I'll send someone to get them for you." He jumped over two dogs wrestling in the dirt, then stalked down the alley. Two women hurried indoors as he passed.

"How do you know him?" Safiyah asked her grandmother, who sat panting on the bench with her stick across her lap.

"Word gets around about boys like him. The Blade. Rasul. Whatever he calls himself." Cucu glared up at Safiyah. "If you go near him again, my stick will find a nice home across your backside." She held her bunched rag to her mouth and spat into it. "I've heard he has big ideas, that boy," she said. "And none of them any good. But you know what they say: 'The hyena cannot smell its own stench.'"

Hyenas used to lurk around the edge of the village with their mean smiles. Not at all like this tall, proud boy, thought Safiyah. "Why is he called Blade if his real name is Rasul?" she asked.

"I shudder to think," said Cucu. "Although I can guess." She peered hard at Safiyah. "What pictures was he talking about?"

"The ones I showed you yesterday," said Safiyah. "I'm going to put them on the walls. On the outside, where everyone can see them."

Cucu picked up the stack of paper from the bench. "Make do with these then." She shoved them into Safiyah's hand. "I won't have you getting pictures— or anything else—from that boy. You stay away from him." She put one hand to her chest and slumped onto her bench with her eyes closed.

Safiyah stood looking down at her grandmother.

She was going to have to tell someone soon about the blood that floated around the bowl she emptied into the gutter every morning. And the streaks of red on the rag Cucu stuffed into her pocket so quickly after her coughing fits.

Safiyah sat down heavily next to her grandmother. Even though she squeezed her eyes shut, a tear leaked out. It crept down her cheek and dropped onto her neck. When she felt her grandmother's hand cover hers, Safiyah held on tight, wishing that was enough to keep them both safe.

Chapter Six

After school Pendo brought two pairs of scissors and a big jar of paste. "I told you Mr. Littlejohn would lend them to us," she told Safiyah. "He told me it's called a collage when you put bits of paper together to make a picture. When you put a collage on a wall, it's a mural."

Lucky Pendo, learning so many things at school, thought Safiyah.

Between taking care of Cucu and doing chores, it took Safiyah three days to finish stuffing paper into all the cracks indoors before she could paste her pictures on the wall around the doorway outside. First she cut out just the right pieces. Then she spread them across the dirt floor of the shack to plan how to put them together.

"Cucu!" she protested each time her grandmother stepped on them. "You're leaving footprints." Cucu was often in a hurry to relieve herself in the ditch, and then too weary to respond as she hauled herself back to bed. When Safiyah asked if she should put a blue picture next to a green or a brown one, her grandmother hardly looked at them. "You're the artful one," she said. "You decide."

As the mural started to grow, more and more people stopped to look at it. One day two small boys sat in the dirt to watch Safiyah work. When their friend came along, they made him stop and look too. Mrs. Simon peered at one of the fashion pictures. She ran her finger down the model's red dress while her two little girls giggled shyly behind her. An old man carrying a can of water on his shoulder muttered, "What nonsense is this?" before he trudged away.

The sun was hot on Safiyah's back as she used up the last picture. Squinting at the glossy paper all day had given her a headache.

Cucu had felt well enough today to play mancala with their neighbor, Mrs. Okella. All morning Safiyah had heard them gossiping and laughing. The game was one of the few things Cucu had brought with her from the village. Each dip in the wooden board was shiny from use. The bag of stones always lived in her pocket. Each time Cucu tucked the mancala board back under the bed, she talked about playing with Safiyah's mother outside their village hut in the evening while baby Safiyah rocked in a tree hammock overhead.

Sometimes Safiyah loved hearing stories about life before they came to Kibera. At other times, it hurt to be reminded of all the people and things they had left behind and how everything had changed.

The only special thing Safiyah still had from those happier times was a braided bracelet. It was twisted and thin now, mended with string she had found at the garbage dump. She remembered her mother making the bracelet for her as the sun went down and the chickens pecked around her feet.

Maybe it wasn't a real memory but just what Cucu called "wishful thinking."

Safiyah fingered her bracelet as she walked slowly along the wall. She peeled away one picture. She slathered more paste on the back and stuck it back in a different spot. The mural did not even cover one wall yet. She needed more pictures if she was going to paper the whole house.

Cucu could be hours with Mrs. Okella. Once they got together, the two old ladies forgot everything except their game.

Safiyah tucked the paste jar under Cucu's bench. Then, with a quick glance at the neighbor's house, she headed down the street toward the garbage dump.

Chapter Seven

Near the railroad tracks, Safiyah dodged around a tangle of writhing and snapping dogs. Up the bank, a crowd of boys chased a train, waving and jeering at the passengers who stared down from the windows. The grinding wheels blew garbage and smelly fumes into the air.

When she caught sight of the little boy who had tried to steal her magazines, Safiyah turned away. But she was not quick enough.

"Hey, girl." He pranced in front of her. "Are you going back for more pictures?"

Safiyah tried to dodge around him. She was glad to see that his friends had not noticed her.

The boy darted to the side so quickly, he was right in front of her again. He had no front teeth.

The blue T-shirt that hung down almost to his bare feet had white writing scrawled across it. "Is that your team?" Safiyah asked. Lots of kids had the names of soccer teams on their shirts. Whenever a big game was playing, the roar of the crowds on the radio and the cheers and taunts of Kibera soccer fans echoed through the alleys.

The boy peered down at himself. "I borrowed it from my cousin." He giggled. "He doesn't mind." He danced around her. "Are you going up the garbage hill again? What did you do with the pictures?"

She stuck her chin in the air and kept walking.

"My name's Chidi. What's yours?" The boy did not bother to wait for an answer. "If you find pictures of cars, can I have them? Or if I help, will you pay me?"

Chidi was like a pesky mosquito, buzzing around and around, but never landing, Safiyah thought. He walked backward ahead of her until he tripped over. He scrambled to his feet and grabbed her arm. "We can get much more if we look together."

She shook him off. "You are a noisy brat."

The dump rose far above Safiyah. From down here, it reminded her of a dead dog she'd once seen in an alley, crawling with maggots and bugs. Hordes of people and birds rooted through the garbage. Adults and children dug with sticks and held things up to look at before throwing them back down or stuffing them in their pockets. Today, the man who roamed the alleys collecting tins was pulling his loaded cart along behind him. A tin rolled off and stopped at Safiyah's feet. When she bent to pick it up, the man grabbed it. "That's mine," he said. "What's yours is yours and what's mine is mine." His eyes flashed as he laughed.

Chidi giggled. "That's what Rasul says," he told Safiyah. "But he says that what's mine is his, and what's his is his too." He plucked at his shirt. "But I got this off him, didn't I?" He giggled.

"Is he your cousin? Blade?" asked Safiyah. "Are you in his gang?"

"He says I'm too small." Chidi pulled himself up straight and tucked his chin into his chest. "I'm not small, am I?"

"You're quite big," she said. She knew that even runty things like Chidi did not like to think of themselves as little.

"I'm not allowed to call my cousin that name," Chidi told her "I live with him and my uncle and aunt.

He had a sister but she died." He wiped his thin wrist across his dripping nose.

Safiyah could not bear to hear about anyone else dying: first her father, when she was just a baby, and then her mother so soon after they arrived in Kibera. Now this little boy's cousin. Safiyah scrambled onto the garbage dump and away from the little boy as fast as she could.

"Wait for me!" called Chidi.

Safiyah did not stop or slow down. But Chidi stuck close as she headed for the place where she had found the magazines yesterday. She tried to ignore the gusts of stinking wind as she climbed higher and higher. Although Chidi kept up an endless stream of chatter, Safiyah did not bother trying to make him go away. She knew he would come buzzing back again just like a mosquito.

A flock of birds soared and screeched above her head. At each step, something crunched under her feet or rolled away. The stench of rotting garbage stuck in the back of her throat. The hazy air made her eyes sting as she headed for a bright patch of red. But it was just an old cloth, torn and ragged and stinking of smoke. Nearby lay a wad of sopping wet newspaper, the print all smudged. It might do for stuffing into the holes in the walls, but today she wanted pictures for her mural.

Safiyah yanked a metal bar out of the garbage. She used it to help her climb across gullies of swampy water and oil, over heaps of tangled old clothes.

Only the tiniest children were up this high. They raked through the garbage, calling back and forth to each other whenever they found something. Their voices sounded like the birds gathered on the power lines along the train tracks, and in the branches that hung over her house in the village.

Safiyah stared into the distance. If she looked hard enough perhaps she could see all the way to her village. If she were a bird, how easy it would be to fly home again.

But she wasn't a bird. And between here and the home she missed so much were the crowded shacks of the slum and the endless maze of buildings and alleys of Nairobi. Beyond Nairobi were roads that ran in all directions, like dark snakes.

"How about this?" Chidi held up a magazine cover with *TIME* written in big white letters across a man's forehead. "That's Mr. President of America,"

Chidi told Safiyah as he handed it to her. He bent down to pull another handful from under a broken box.

After lots of digging and sorting, Chidi and Safiyah had as many old magazines as they could carry. As the sun glared overhead, they clambered back down, each holding armfuls of paper.

Safiyah was very thirsty. She looked around, but there was nowhere to buy water, even if she could pay for it. A big square can stood outside a hut. She dunked one hand in to scoop up some water but before she could bring it to her mouth, her hand was knocked aside. "Hey!" Water splashed onto her legs and made dark marks as it landed on the dirt.

Blade glared down at her. His face shone with sweat and his eyes flashed.

Chapter Eight

"Why did you do that?" asked Safiyah. "I'm thirsty."

"You should know not to drink water unless you know it's clean, you stupid girl."

She stepped backward. "Stay away from me."

Blade grinned down at her. "I've been looking for this scrawny thing everywhere." He grabbed Chidi's shirt and hauled him off the ground. The little boy's legs dangled in the air. "Why aren't you in school?" he asked.

"I'm going, Rasul. I am," said Chidi.

"He followed me," Safiyah told Rasul. "He's a pest."

"See. Everyone thinks you're a pest," Rasul told Chidi as he gave him a shake.

"Let me go!" Chidi kicked his feet as he tried to get free.

"Do I have to take you to school myself?" his cousin asked.

"I'm going." Chidi squirmed out of Rasul's grasp, dropped to the ground and raced away without looking back.

Safiyah watched him go. She knew she should run away too. But instead, she asked, "Why do they call you Blade?"

Chidi's cousin frowned down at her. He rapped her shoulder with his hard knuckles. "Don't call me that! I'm Rasul to you."

"Don't you go to school?" Safiyah asked. She knew she shouldn't be talking to him, but she couldn't help herself.

"I could ask you the same thing," he said.

"I take care of my cucu."

"Not taking care of her now, are you?" Rasul frowned. "What's wrong with her?" he asked.

"I don't know." Safiyah poked her foot in the dirt. She swallowed hard. "She coughs a lot." Her voice dropped to a whisper. "She's been coughing blood."

"What?"

"When she coughs, she coughs up blood." Safiyah glared at Rasul. "I tried to keep out the nighttime cold by stuffing paper in all the holes. But there is still blood when she coughs." She tried to hold the words back, but they kept coming. "What if she has AIDS like my mother?" She swiped at her wet face. "Lots of people get sick here. And we have no money. That's why I don't go to school. No money for school." She shoved her fist in her eyes, trying to push back the tears. "Or for medicine."

Rasul bent down and peered at her. "How old are you anyway?"

Safiyah gulped. "Ten."

Rasul grabbed her arm.

"Wait!" She tried to pull away. He walked so fast she had to run to keep up. "Help!" she cried.

The dark alley Rasul dragged her through was so narrow they had to run sideways. Here, there was no one dozing in the shade or carrying bundles of clothes to the washhouse. No one to stop her from being kidnapped by a gang leader. "Where are you taking me?" Safiyah pulled back as hard as she could. Rasul stopped so suddenly she slammed into his side.

"You said you were thirsty." He glared at her. "I will get you something to drink." He tightened his grip on Safiyah's arm and hurried on. "Then we will take care of your grandmother."

Chapter Nine

Just when Safiyah thought she would faint if she had to run any farther, Rasul pulled her out into bright daylight. Here, the houses were not so close together. There were even patches of garden outside some, with enough room to hang clothes to dry in the sun.

A woman stood in the doorway of a shack wearing a long traditional *kitenge* dress and a bright shawl. "You seem to have brought home the wrong child," she said to Rasul.

He pushed Safiyah forward. "Ma, this is Safiyah. Can we give her a drink?"

"Where's Chidi?" the woman asked as she poured water from an enamel jug into a jar and held it out to Safiyah.

Safiyah watched Rasul's mother over the rim as she drank.

"At school by now," said Rasul.

Safiyah handed back the empty jar. "Thank you."

"I'm Grace Pakua." The woman's hand was cool as she shook Safiyah's. "Pleased to meet you, child. Where did you find your cousin this time?" she asked Rasul.

"Guess."

Mrs. Pakua shook her head. "At the dump again, I suppose." She looked closely at Safiyah. "I'm sure you know to stay away from that dangerous place."

Before Safiyah could decide whether to lie or tell the truth, Rasul told his mother, "Safiyah's cucu is sick. Can you take a look at her?" He turned to Safiyah. "Mother works at the clinic."

"Just as a cleaner," Mrs. Pakua told her. "Have you taken your grandmother to see the doctors there?"

"It's too far for her to walk," Safiyah answered. "And we don't have any money."

"The clinic is free."

"Oh," said Safiyah. She hadn't known that. "But if she needs medicine. Or has to stay in hospital…"

"Perhaps you are worried about being home alone. You would be able to stay with your cucu if they needed to keep her there for treatment. Lots of patients' families stay with them at the clinic. And only those who can afford it have to pay." Mrs. Pakua adjusted her head scarf and took Safiyah's hand. "But let's not imagine the worst. Rasul, I am going to take this child home to see what we can do for her cucu."

"Good. I've got things to do." Without saying goodbye, Rasul turned and disappeared back into the alley.

His mother stood beside Safiyah as they watched him hurry away. Safiyah had never thought about gang members having mothers!

"Is it just the two of you?" asked Mrs. Pakua.

Safiyah nodded.

"You look after your grandmother, I expect."

Safiyah nodded again.

"Let's see what I can do to help." Mrs. Pakua moved as quickly as Rasul, but her hand on Safiyah's was gentler. "We'll go this way." As she led Safiyah through the neighborhood, Mrs. Pakua talked about the clinic, telling Safiyah how good the doctors and nurses were, even with so little equipment and medicine.

As if Mrs. Pakua realized that all the talk about doctors and medicine was making Safiyah nervous, she squeezed her hand. "Whatever is wrong with your grandmother, we will find help for her."

Mrs. Pakua greeted many people as she led Safiyah through the maze of unfamiliar alleys. They passed tea shops and newspaper stands. The women filling their wash buckets at the standpipe waved and called out to her. Not everyone in Kibera washed their clothes in dirty ditch water, Safiyah realized. Not everyone was as poor as she was.

When they at last turned the corner at the familiar water vendor's stand, they found the alley full of people stumbling through a blue haze of smoke. At first Safiyah could not make any sense of the words in the hubbub of voices. But then she heard, "Not enough water."

"Let us pass! Let us pass!"

A man pushed past Safiyah and Mrs. Pakua. His hair was singed and a dark smudge ran down his face. "More water!" he cried.

A flash of panic swept across Safiyah's chest. "My house is along there." She let go of Mrs. Pakua's hand and pushed through the crowds. She ducked between two men and raced past a crush of uniformed children being led away by an old man.

"Pendo!" cried Safiyah.

Her friend's face turned toward her above a sea of heads. "It's a fire!" Pendo waved wildly above the crowd of children pressed against her. "Saffy! A fire at Mrs. Okella's."

Chapter Ten

Fire! Mrs. Okella! Pendo's words pounded in Safiyah's head as she shoved through the crowd. Fire! "Let me through." She stepped on someone's foot. An elbow banged the back of her head. A basket scraped against her bare legs. "I need to find my cucu," she yelled.

Two church elders held back the crowds outside Mrs. Okella's house. Their clothes were blackened and torn and their faces shone with sweat. The burning walls of the house were crumpled in on each other. Sticking out from underneath was a table leg and a tangle of fabric.

"Cucu!" cried Safiyah.

A woman grabbed her shoulder. "Is that your house?"

"My cucu…" Safiyah sobbed.

"This child lives over there," the woman called to the people who filled the narrow alley. "Her grandmother…"

"That's my house." Safiyah pointed next door. Her wall of pictures was blistered and peeling. Ashes swirled in the air. "Where's Cucu?" Safiyah screamed, just as she had screamed the day she had found her mother in a heap in this very spot.

"I thought I had lost you." Rasul's mother was beside Safiyah.

"Cucu!" wailed Safiyah as Mrs. Pakua held her tight.

Men scooped water from the ditches and hurried toward the house. Others kicked the rubble as the flames flickered through heaps of scorched wood and paper. Safiyah saw a woman tuck Mrs. Okella's blanket under her own shawl and hurry away.

"I have to go in," screamed Safiyah. "I have to see my grandmother. She was visiting Mrs. Okella."

"The house is empty," said the man who was trying to keep people away.

All the noise and bustle seemed to fade away. "What do you mean?" Her voice sounded like it came from a long way away.

"Everyone on this side of the alley was sent away until the fire is put out."

"Come with me, child," said Mrs. Pakua.

"No. Let me see." Safiyah rushed past the man. She raced over the littered ground, ignoring voices behind her and arms reaching out to stop her.

The curtain over her doorway was burned and ragged. But inside, the bed was tidily made. Her grandmother's knitting basket was safe on the shelf. The house smelled of smoke and an unnatural heat came through one wall.

Nothing was burned. But the house was empty.

Safiyah dashed outside again, right into Mrs. Pakua's arms. "Cucu's not there!"

Mrs. Pakua turned to one of the church elders. "Where have the neighbors gone?"

He pointed down the lane. "Everyone is at Zuma's bicycle shop until this street is safe."

A woman hurried forward and whispered to the man.

His face was very serious as he turned back to Safiyah and Rasul's mother. "The news is not good." He studied the thick black smoke rising from the burned house. "It seems we were not able to save Mrs. Okella."

Safiyah pulled on Rasul's mother's hands. "What does he mean?" But she could read the answer in her eyes. Mrs. Okella was dead. "I must find Cucu." Safiyah's scream spiraled into the air. "Where is my cucu?" The crowd moved aside to let her pass.

The alley was usually filled with shouts and laughter, with the sound of crying babies and barking dogs. But now Safiyah heard only the blood pounding in her ears as she ran to find the only person she had left in the world.

Chapter Eleven

Safiyah found her grandmother asleep on a crate, leaning against a cluttered counter at the back of the bicycle shop. It was very dark, and smelled of oil and sweat and tobacco smoke. "Cucu?"

Her grandmother opened her eyes slowly.

"Cucu!"

"There you are, my little one." Cucu pulled Safiyah onto her lap. She patted Safiyah's back as she gulped and hiccupped. She stroked Safiyah's cheek as she groped for the words to tell her about Mrs. Okella.

"That poor, poor lady." Cucu eased Safiyah aside. She pulled the little cloth bag that bulged with mancala stones from her pocket. "She was so happy to win this time." She heaved herself to her feet. "Now you are here, we will go home."

"I couldn't find you," wailed Safiyah. She started shaking again. "I thought you were dead!"

Cucu pulled Safiyah back against her thin body. "After Mrs. Okella won her game, I came home. But you were gone. I came looking for you." She patted her chest. "Mr. Zuma found me coughing and brought me here." She looked around the crowded shop. Two babies slept on their mother's shoulders. A group of men smoked as they talked quietly together. A family sat against a wall without speaking. "We were both lost, for a little while," said Cucu. She stood with one hand resting against the bench. Beads of sweat dotted her forehead and her lips were dry and cracked. She put a fist to her mouth and began coughing.

"You see?" Safiyah said to Mrs. Pakua, who had waited silently as Safiyah was reunited with her grand-mother. The old worry about losing the only family she had left rose in Safiyah like a gust of wind.

"Perhaps you should rest a little longer." Mrs. Pakua helped Cucu sit down. "I am Grace Pakua," she told her. "You granddaughter's new friend."

"I know of your family." Cucu scrabbled in her pocket for her rag. She wiped her mouth. "I met Rasul the other day. Blade as he calls himself."

"Rasul," said Mrs. Pakua quietly and firmly. "His name is Rasul."

Cucu struggled to stand. "Thank you for your help. But as you can see, my Saffy will take good care of her old cucu."

"Perhaps you need more help than she can provide," Mrs. Pakua said. She quickly added, "It may not yet be safe for you to return to your own home."

"Cucu," begged Safiyah. "You should go to the clinic. Your coughing…"

"It is nothing," said Cucu.

"Cucu!" Safiyah's voice was so loud that the crowd of people filling Mr. Zuma's shop turned to stare.

Safiyah bent closer to her grandmother. "You are sick." Her chin trembled as she searched for the right words. "If you get more sick…if you die, I will have no one." Mrs. Pakua's warm hand on the back of her neck gave her the courage to go on. "I can't take care of everything." She leaned against her grandmother. "Please, Cucu," she begged. She tried to swallow the tears that rose in her throat. "I want you to be well so you can look after *me*."

Tears ran down the long creases of her grandmother's face as she nodded slowly. "Of course you do, my child. Of course you do." Cucu wiped her own face with her rag, then dabbed at Safiyah's tears. She looked closely at Safiyah, her eyes shimmering. She turned to Mrs. Pakua. "I would be very grateful for your help."

Safiyah leaned against her grandmother and felt her thin arms hold her tight.

"Mr. Zuma will let you rest here a little longer, I am sure," Rasul's mother said. "I will find someone to bring you tea. And as soon as I have seen what arrangements can be made for your care, I will return."

For just a moment, in her brightly colored kitenge, Mrs. Pakua reminded Safiyah of her mother who, a long time ago and far from here, had stood in the doorway of their village house waiting for Safiyah to come home.

Rasul's mother lifted her hand and waved. "I won't be long," she called. Then she was gone.

Chapter Twelve

For more than a week, Safiyah hardly left the clinic. It was a noisy and busy place. The nurses and doctors were kind. And tucked against Cucu's side at night, Safiyah was able to stop worrying so much about her grandmother. Once the nurses reassured her that Cucu would be treated for free, Safiyah relaxed, and enjoyed watching everything going on around them.

While her grandmother spent long hours sleeping, Safiyah studied the doctors hurrying between patients and discussing their care. She got to know many of the other families and played with small children who got bored sitting on their mother's laps. She fetched water and folded blankets. She cooled hot faces with damp cloths. She held basins of water while the nurses cleaned wounds.

When a doctor let her wear his stethoscope around her neck for a little while, she thought that perhaps she might grow up to work in a clinic.

Mrs. Pakua came to see Cucu every evening after work, and Chidi sometimes came on his way home from school. But he was soon sent away for getting in the way. When Safiyah asked if Rasul might come to visit, his mother simply said he was busy.

Each day Cucu's cough got a little better. She began to sleep less and soon there was no blood in the white bowl that Safiyah emptied each morning.

One afternoon her grandmother patted the blanket. "Come here."

Safiyah cuddled up close.

"I've watched you," said Cucu. "So helpful. Now can you do something for me?"

Safiyah jumped to her feet. "Shall I tidy your bed?"

"I am quite comfortable." Cucu patted Safiyah's arm. "But I worry about our house."

"Mrs. Pakua says everything is fine," Safiyah told her grandmother.

"She is so kind. But you know what I miss?"

"Your mancala board?" suggested Safiyah.

When Cucu nodded, her face was sad. "I may have left it at Mrs. Okella's house. Or perhaps I took it home. I forget so much. Will you find it for me?"

"Your stones are here," Safiyah told her. "Safe under the mattress."

"I would like to know the board is safe too." Cucu's eyes were brighter now and her cheeks were not as shadowy. But what if she got sick again while Safiyah was away on this errand?

As if she knew what Safiyah was thinking, Cucu said, "You don't have to worry about me, Saffy. And I know it's just a little thing, but my mancala board is all I have."

Safiyah fingered her own bracelet.

"Can you do this for me?" asked Cucu.

First Safiyah filled her grandmother's cup at the tap. Cucu sipped and handed it back. Then Safiyah tucked the blanket tighter around her grandmother's thin legs. "Hurry now." Cucu smiled. "I will be right here. Waiting for you."

After one long look back, Safiyah pushed through the families crowded between the patients' beds and chatting on the porch. She stepped over children playing in the courtyard while more sick people sat in the shade, waiting to a see doctor.

It seemed so long since she had come here with Cucu. And in such a panic. For a moment Safiyah could not remember how to get home.

Then she heard the roar of a train in the distance. She saw the power lines that ran along the tracks. She followed them along the bank where boys played in the rubble and dogs fought over garbage. She passed the stall selling water bottles and roasted corn nuts.

Back on familiar streets, she hurried past the customers lined up at the water vendor. She waved to Mr. Zuma, who was turning a bicycle tire in a bucket of water.

A new shack of boards and iron sheets stood where Mrs. Okella's house had been. Two children played outside with a bucket while their mother chatted to an old man leaning on a stick.

Cucu's bench was just where it belonged, outside the house Safiyah shared with her grandmother. And behind it was the wall that Safiyah had last seen all smudged and blistered from the fire.

But now it was covered once again in bright pictures.

Chapter Thirteen

"How is your grandmother, child?" Safiyah's new neighbor asked as she tucked her hair into her scarf.

"Better, thank you," answered Safiyah. "Have you...? I mean, who has been here?"

"Such a good friend you have. She comes almost every day straight from school."

"Pendo did this?"

"I believe that is her name. You are very lucky to have such a good friend." The woman bent to pick up a child. "Let me know if your cucu needs help when she comes home."

Safiyah went indoors. The small space felt stuffy and hot. A fly flicked from one wall to the other above her head.

Safiyah found her grandmother's mancala board on the bed where she must have left it. She tucked it tightly under her arm. They had so little. But she still had her bracelet. And her grandmother had her precious game.

Outside, Safiyah sat on Cucu's bench to wait for Pendo. She ran her fingers along the wooden board, remembering how quickly the fire had taken Mrs. Okella's house and her few belongings. How lucky the fire had not spread to her house and stolen the few reminders of their old life.

A crowd of school children turned the corner. "Saffy!" Pendo ran toward her. "I have missed you so much."

When Pendo reached to hug her, Safiyah moved aside and pointed at the wall. "Did you do this?" she asked.

Pendo grinned. "Aren't you surprised?"

"It's all wrong," said Safiyah.

Pendo's smile faded. "I thought you'd be pleased."

"I am. I mean, thank you. But I was…There's a pattern."

"What do you mean, a pattern? It's just color. Lots of different colors and shapes." Pendo dropped her schoolbag on the ground and ran her hand across the wall. "There is hardly any space between the pictures. I was very careful." She frowned. "I did it for you, Saffy."

"But there has to be a pattern. A design," insisted Safiyah. "It's a mural, Pendo. Like Mr. Littlejohn said. It is not just pieces of paper."

"You're jealous." Pendo's voice was thin and hard. "I got the scissors and the paste. I finished it myself. You are mad because I did it and you didn't."

The two girls stood facing each other on the busy street.

Safiyah wanted to be grateful, she really did. Pendo had done just what Safiyah had set out to do. To cover the outside of the shack with bright color now that she had filled in the cracks in the walls inside to keep out the cold and the heat, the smoke and the smells. But as her mural had grown, a picture had taken shape in her head. A picture of something new and fresh out of something old and thrown away.

This wall of color and shapes was nothing like the picture in her head.

Safiyah yanked a loose piece of paper away from the wall. As she pulled, the strip grew and grew, leaving a long scar. She reached forward again.

"Don't!" Pendo stepped in front of Safiyah. "You spoiled it!"

"You're the one who spoiled it." Safiyah pushed her friend aside.

Pendo tripped against the edge of Cucu's bench. "That hurt!"

When Safiyah reached out to help her up, Pendo pushed her hand away. "I don't need to be sticking bits of silly paper on an old wall anyway. I have lots of other friends. We have much more interesting things to do." Without another word, she ran down the alley, turned the corner and was out of sight.

Safiyah looked at the ragged piece of paper hanging from her fingers. She crumpled it up and dropped it on the ground.

When she looked at the wall, all she could see through her tears was a blur of colors and shapes that made no sense at all.

Chapter Fourteen

Cucu was asleep when Safiyah got back to the clinic. Families were crowded between the beds, sharing food, talking and laughing. One lady who stayed at the clinic to take care of her son handed Safiyah a bean cake as she passed.

She broke it in half and set one piece on Cucu's blanket, then sat cross-legged on the end of the bed and watched her grandmother's chest rise and fall. Her eyelids fluttered as if she was dreaming. Safiyah crumbled her piece of bean cake into pieces and dropped them into the dips in the mancala board.

Mrs. Pakua emerged through the crowd and looked down at Cucu. "How is your cucu today?" she asked.

"Better, I think." Safiyah ducked her head.

"How are you?"

"I'm all right." Safiyah stared at her lap.

The bed squeaked as Mrs. Pakua sat down, careful not to disturb Safiyah's grandmother. She touched Safiyah's cheeks with her finger. "Are those tears?"

"I had a fight with my friend," Safiyah told her.

"I am sure you can soon make up."

"She doesn't need me." Safiyah gulped. "She has lots of other friends at school."

"I expect you'd like to go to school."

Safiyah chewed her lip. There was no point in answering.

"Chidi can go to school," said Mrs. Pakua with a laugh. "But he would rather stay home."

"Blade doesn't go to school," said Safiyah.

"Rasul. We call him by his proper name." Mrs. Pakua's voice was sad. "No, Rasul doesn't go to school anymore."

"People are scared of him," said Safiyah. "But he is kind to me."

Mrs. Rasul's eyes filled with tears. "Rasul likes you too." She stroked Safiyah's cheek. "You remind him…you remind us…" she stammered. She took a breath and smiled sadly at Safiyah. "His sister was your age when she died," she said. "We all miss her."

Safiyah wanted to slap her hands against her ears. She didn't want to hear anything more about people dying. About people losing their mothers or fathers. Or their little girls.

She struggled to think of the right thing to say. But the words got all mixed up in a tangle of anger and sadness. Finally she asked quietly, "What was her name?"

Mrs. Pakua blinked. A tear trickled down her cheek and dropped onto her bright kitenge. "Arafa. Her name was Arafa." A smile quivered on her lips. "Do you know what that means?"

"No."

"It means *intelligent*. Arafa was a bright spark in our lives. She loved school."

She patted Safiyah's knee. "As I am sure you will. One day."

Safiyah fingered the crumbs in Cucu's mancala board. How could that ever happen? she wondered. "Rasul should be in school," said Mrs. Pakua. "But life here in Kibera is hard for everyone, as you know.

And much of what Rasul and his…gang…" Mrs. Pakua cleared her throat. "I don't like to think of them like that. But that's how everyone thinks of them. Rasul and his friends do many things that I might not approve of. But he takes care of his family." Her voice was low and fierce. "We all need to take care of our families if we are to survive."

"Like my girl here." Cucu was awake.

Safiyah sat quietly as Mrs. Pakua helped Cucu sit up. There was so much to think about. Blade's—Rasul's—sister. Survival. Taking care of each other.

"I am pleased to see you looking so much better," Mrs. Pakua told Cucu.

"I feel better," said Cucu. "I think it is time I went home. Did you bring what I asked?" she asked Safiyah.

As Safiyah held up the mancala board, crumbs trickled onto the blanket. She gathered them in her hand before Cucu saw her wasting food.

"This is one of the few things that we brought with us from our village," Cucu told Mrs. Pakua. "Saffy. Hand me my stones."

Safiyah pulled them out from under the mattress, where she had tucked them days ago. The stones rattled as she emptied the bag onto the blankets.

Mrs. Pakua picked one up. "So pretty."

"Shall I play with you, Cucu?" asked Safiyah.

"You?" Her grandmother frowned at her. "It is a game for old ladies, you said. Boring."

"I changed my mind. I want you to teach me."

Cucu grinned as she found a flat place in the blankets to set her mancala board.

Mrs. Pakua stood up. "I will leave you to your game. But first I want to speak with the doctor. Later, Rasul will bring you supper."

"Send the little boy too," said Cucu. "I forget my troubles when he is around."

Safiyah watched Mrs. Pakua step between the patients and their families, who filled the ward. She held the mancala stones in her hand, ready to play a game that her mother and grandmother had shared in a village that seemed farther and farther away every day.

Chapter Fifteen

By the time Cucu was ready to leave the clinic, her cough had almost gone. The shadows around her eyes were not so deep and her skin was cool and dry.

The clamor of the ward was familiar to Safiyah now. She liked the strange smells, the quiet voices in the night, and the constant flow of people in and out. She was also glad to be going home again, to the scent of supper fires along the alley, the neighbors' loud laughter and the rattle of kettles at the tea shop.

Safiyah helped Cucu straighten her dress. She pinned her grandmother's little package of pills inside her T-shirt along with the note of when Cucu should take them. The doctor said her grandmother would need them for a long time. Every day at the right time.

Safiyah would have to ask someone to read the note. Perhaps, if Pendo came by…

She helped her grandmother slip on her shoes, taking care not to hurt her bunions, then handed Cucu her stick.

Her grandmother's hand shook as she leaned against Safiyah's shoulder while they made their way slowly through the ward. Some patients and their families called out goodbye while others waved weakly from their beds.

In the doorway, Cucu stood blinking in the bright sunlight.

The few coins a nurse had given them for the bus were sweaty in Safiyah's hand, and the bus stop was a long way away. Safiyah studied the ground to make sure there was nothing to trip over as she led her grandmother into the street.

"Were you not going to wait for me?" asked Rasul. How often he seemed to appear out of thin air! "Let me guess." He grinned. "I bet the little pest did not tell you."

"Little pest?" asked Cucu.

"Chidi, of course. He was supposed to tell you that I would be here after I had checked it out with my boss."

"Your boss?" asked Cucu. "You have a job?"

"I am going to learn to fix cars."

"Cars! Perhaps if I had stayed longer, you could have driven us home!" said Cucu with a laugh. Safiyah expected her grandmother to start coughing. But Cucu just said, "Cars!" again, and slipped her arm through Rasul's. She handed Safiyah her stick and held on to her elbow on the other side.

It took a long time to reach the bus stop. As they waited in the noise and fumes of the street, three boys Rasul's age whispered to each other and crossed to the other side. An old man waiting for the bus muttered something under his breath and spat on the ground.

Rasul ignored them all.

Safiyah thought of all the questions she wanted to ask but decided to keep to herself. He might be Blade to other people and to boys in his gang, but he was a good friend to her and her grandmother. It was all about survival, his mother said. And she and Cucu needed friends if they were to survive in Kibera.

At last the bus came, billowing smoke and grinding its gears. Rasul settled Cucu into a seat between a woman nursing a baby and an old man with a basket on his lap. A chicken flapped and squawked inside.

Safiyah stood in the aisle beside Rasul, jostled by the noisy crush of people. Some stared at Rasul and Safiyah. Others avoided looking at them at all.

Safiyah felt shy, thinking about what Rasul's mother had told her about Arafa. Was that the reason Rasul was so kind to her? Did she remind him of his little sister?

As they lurched along the dusty road, Safiyah thought of the last time she had been on a bus, on the long journey to the city. Just like last time, she was so hemmed in by sweaty bodies and bulging bags and bundles she could hardly see out the windows.

At last the bus stopped and Rasul led them along the crowded aisle. He got down first, then turned and wrapped his arms around Cucu. She laughed as he swung her to the ground. Safiyah watched them from the top of the steps.

"Better come quick," said Rasul.

Safiyah leaped down just as the bus started moving again.

While Cucu leaned on her stick and watched the bus rattle away, Safiyah looked around her. The sign over Mr. Zuma's shop swung in the hot breeze. A brown dog slept in the sun. A jar of flowers stood outside a house, and a broken chair covered with drying clothes leaned against a wall. A raggedy line of neighbors waited at the water vendor's stand.

This was home now, thought Safiyah. Even if it would never feel the same as her village.

Safiyah and Rasul walked beside Cucu as they made their way home. At their doorway, Cucu smiled at the colorful mural. "How lovely!" she said.

Rasul hardly glanced at the house as he helped her inside.

Safiyah stared at the ragged space on the wall where she had torn away Pendo's pictures. She slumped down onto Cucu's bench. Shreds of torn paper and ashes drifted around her legs as she scuffed her feet in the dirt.

She kicked harder as all the anger at her friend came sweeping back, like a bad smell through a crack in the wall.

"Saffy!" called Cucu.

"What?"

"Come here, child."

Cucu sat on the bed with her back against the wall. Her thin legs stuck out from beneath her skirt. "Take off my shoes for me, would you?"

Rasul watched Safiyah settle Cucu. "I will be right back," he said.

When Rasul had gone, Cucu asked Safiyah, "Did we forget my mancala board at the hospital?"

"I have it here." Safiyah turned around to show where she had tucked it in the waistband of her shorts.

"Clever girl," said Cucu.

Safiyah placed the board on the bed next to her grandmother.

"It will be yours when I die," Cucu told her.

"Don't say that!"

Cucu patted Safiyah's hand. "But not for a long time." She took the bag of stones from her pocket and tipped them into her open hand. "Not for many years."

"Do you want to play now?" asked Safiyah.

"Not today. I am a little tired," said Cucu. "You may borrow it if you are careful not to break it. Or lose the stones. Perhaps Pendo might like to play with you."

"Pendo is not my friend anymore," Safiyah told her.

"Not your friend?"

"She spoiled my paper wall," Safiyah told her grandmother.

"It looks lovely," said Cucu. "Even with my old eyes."

"When I was away, she slapped everything up," Safiyah shouted at her grandmother. "I had a plan. Now it's just a jumble."

"Would you lose a friend who tried to help?" Cucu's voice was full of disappointment.

The springs squealed as Safiyah slumped onto the bed.

"Come here," said Cucu.

Safiyah shifted close. She breathed in the dusky smell of her grandmother's skin mixed with the tang of the clinic soap.

"We are so lucky to make some new friends, Saffy," said Cucu. "Mrs. Pakua has been so kind. Many neighbors came to visit us in the clinic." She ran her hand up and down Safiyah's arm. "One should never judge a friend who tries to help."

Safiyah quoted one of her grandmother's favorite proverbs. "'Words are easy. Friendship is hard.' You told me that."

"So you do listen to your old cucu." Cucu tapped Safiyah's hand. "It means that you should work hard to keep the good friends you have. And take care that your words do not drive them away."

Cucu slumped against the wall. She was better, but she still tired easily. Safiyah helped her lie down and draped the thin blanket over her.

She looked around. The shack was already cozier, but with the cracks filled, it was dim in here, even though it was still daylight outside. "We will have to use the lamp more now," she said. "And how will we pay for the oil?"

Cucu hand reached out to slap Safiyah's leg. "Go away if you wish to sulk. We are home. I am almost well. With so little, is that not enough?" She turned her face to the wall. "Now let me rest."

Chapter Sixteen

Safiyah barged out of the house, straight into Rasul. Water slopped onto her leg from the can he was carrying.

"Looks like you needed a wash." He laughed.

Safiyah darted past him without answering.

"Where are you going?" he called after her.

At the corner of the street she tripped over two children playing in the dirt. She landed with one hand bent underneath her. She held it against her chest and squeezed her eyes shut. But she could not stop the tears.

"Do you want to play?" A little boy with a very dirty face held a tangle of string out to her.

"No!"

"Why are you crying?" the boy asked. "Are you hurt?" Now his friend was staring at her too.

"Mind your own business." Safiyah stood up and wiggled her sore hand back and forth. If it was broken, she might have to go back to the clinic.

She looked back toward her own street. For a moment she wondered if Rasul might come after her. But what would the neighbors think, if they saw a gang leader chasing a little girl?

She looked at the busy streets and alleys ahead of her. Kibera stretched out in all directions, more streets than she would ever know, crowded with more people than she could count.

Pendo and her schoolmates turned the corner, coming her way. Safiyah watched as Pendo strutted along with her nose in the air.

Without planning to, Safiyah reached toward her friend. "Pendo?"

Pendo brushed her hand away. "Do I know you?" Her voice was thin and mean.

"Please…wait…" Safiyah stammered.

Pendo turned her back on Safiyah. She linked arms with another girl and walked away without looking back.

Safiyah stood alone in the middle of the alley with her hands hanging at her side.

Suddenly, her hand was grabbed from behind. "You're home!" Chidi hopped up and down and hung on to her arm. "Is your Cucu dead now? Are you all alone in the world, like me?" He grinned at her, as if he didn't mind one bit.

She shook her sore hand free. "She's not dead! Anyway, you're not alone. You have Rasul, and your aunt and uncle."

Chidi grinned. "Let's go see your cucu. I bet she missed me."

"You were supposed to tell us that Rasul was coming to meet us at the clinic."

"I had to go to school," said Chidi. He giggled.

The little pest reminded Safiyah of the monkeys that hung from the trees in her village. A nuisance, but amusing. She couldn't help smiling. "Don't you know how lucky you are? I wish I could go to school."

"Lucky?" Chidi's grubby fingers circled her arm as he pulled her along the alley. "School is boring. Two times two is four. Two times three is six. Two times four is nine," he chanted. "It's all tables and reading."

Reading! Even Chidi could read! thought Safiyah. "Come on," he called, trotting ahead.

At the house, Chidi darted along the wall. "What's that?" He pointed at the bare slash where Safiyah had torn down Pendo's pictures.

"You ask too many questions." She gave him a little push. "You wanted to see Cucu. So go and say hello to Cucu. But don't wake her if she is sleeping."

Safiyah studied a few pictures that had survived the fire, and others from her collection that Pendo had added. Then in one corner she spotted the picture of the glinting blue swimming pool. The one Pendo had snuck into her pocket.

Pendo had given up her favorite picture! And in return Safiyah had been mean and ungrateful. She leaned forward to flatten a loose piece of paper. Friendship *was* hard, she thought. And words were easy. Sometimes they made it too easy to hurt a good friend.

But finding the right words to make up was going to be hard.

After a supper of Mrs. Pakua's groundnut stew, Safiyah and Cucu played mancala. Safiyah gave Cucu some water to wash down her pills, then wrapped the rest back in their paper and tucked them in the tin under her bed.

She rolled her bracelet off her wrist and put it safely inside too.

"The clinic mattress was better," said Cucu, as she settled down for the night. "But it is nice to be home." Safiyah was sweeping the rug when Cucu added, "Rasul left something under the bed for you."

A cardboard box was pushed among the clutter of pots and dishes. Inside Safiayah found a stack of brightly colored magazine pages. There were pictures of colorful gardens and women in smart clothes. Some showed fancy meals laid out on white tablecloths, while others showed city streets full of people looking in shop windows.

Here were enough pictures to cover a whole wall, thought Safiyah. Perhaps even more.

When she sniffed the paper, Safiyah could smell rotten food and smoke, oil and rancid water and dirty diapers.

It must have taken Rasul a long time to collect all the pictures.

Safiyah grinned. Chidi must have helped. That's why there were no pictures of cars in the pile!

Chapter Seventeen

All the next day, Cucu sat like a queen accepting visitors. Some neighbors came with corn cakes, others with tea. Some stood outside the door chatting while many crowded inside until there was no room for Safiyah.

She spent the hours papering the back wall of the shack.

First she sorted the pictures into colors. She put the greens and blues together, then the yellows and the oranges and browns and the reds. She sorted all the whites and blacks and grays and made a pile of multi-colored pictures. She squinted at the wall, deciding how to arrange them.

The paste was dry around the edges of the jar. But there was still enough. She mixed brown and yellow pictures in a long slash from the bottom corner at one end of the wall to the top of the other end. To reach up high, she stacked an old crate on a chair with a broken leg. She tumbled off twice, but nothing stopped her from working on her mural. By midafternoon, her arms and neck ached.

She shooed away the visitors and gave Cucu her pills. Then she settled her in bed for a rest.

As she waited on the bench, Safiyah practiced what she would say to Pendo when she came by.

She asked neighbors to come back later to visit when Cucu was awake. She smiled at the people she didn't know who stopped to look at the brightly colored wall. She helped a woman pick up a bundle of pots and pans that fell off her head. A huddle of boys in tracksuits dribbled a soccer ball down the street. Three small kids in school uniforms dashed past.

Maybe she had missed Pendo.

Safiyah was about to run indoors to check on Cucu, when Pendo turned the corner. Today, instead of being surrounded by her school friends, she was with a tall white man with red hair. When she saw Safiyah, she ducked her head and said, "My teacher wanted to see what you are doing with the glue and the scissors." She looked at the wall instead of Safiyah, as if she didn't want to be there at all.

Blond hairs peeked from the man's sleeve when he put out his hand to greet Safiyah. "I'm pleased to meet you."

She wiped her hand on her shorts before she shook hands with him. Maybe Mr. Littlejohn had not seen her all those times she hid below the classroom window, watching everyone at work.

He stepped into the middle of the alley while he studied the papered wall. "So this is the project Pendo told me about."

"Yes, sir," said Safiyah.

Pendo glared at her.

Safiyah thought about what Cucu had said about words and friendship. And needing all their friends if they were to survive the hard life in Kibera. She moved closer to Pendo and said to the teacher, "Thank you for lending me the paste and the scissors."

Mr. Littlejohn just nodded and moved closer to study the wall.

Safiyah took a deep breath and added, "Pendo helped me."

Her friend smiled slowly, looking as relived as Safiyah felt. Then Pendo looked sad again for a moment. "But I spoiled Safiyah's design."

"It's okay," said Safiyah. "Look. I started the other wall." She led Mr. Littlejohn and Pendo around the corner.

"It's a road!" said Pendo, pointing.

"You're right," said Mr. Littlejohn. "It looks so hot and dusty with all those browns and yellows. And that patch of blue and green?" He pointed to where the wall met the crooked roof.

"That's my village," Safiyah told him. "Far away in the country."

He nodded. "I see." He scanned the whole wall. "But your mural is not yet finished."

"I have enough pictures for this wall. Maybe one other." Safiyah looked at her friend before she turned back to her teacher. "But I don't have enough paste."

"Paste?" Mr. Littlejohn turned slowly toward both girls as if he had forgotten they were there. "I'm sure I can find you more paste," he said. "Then you can finish this wall. And what will you do on the next one?"

"I don't know yet," said Safiyah. When she saw the hopeful look on her friend's face, she found it easy to say the right words. "Pendo can help me decide. It was her idea to start with."

Chapter Eighteen

"Saffy?" Cucu came round the corner, leaning on her stick. "All this chatter woke me. Who is this?"

"David Littlejohn, missus." He shook hands with Cucu. "Pendo's teacher. She told me all about your granddaughter's mural. You just be very proud of her."

Cucu grinned. "My Safiyah is a good granddaughter."

"And she has such talent." The teacher nodded toward the mural on the back wall.

"Talent?" Cucu frowned. "Saffy does have persistence. The time she has taken…"

"Her work here is…" Mr. Littlejohn groped for the word. "Splendid," he finally said. "In fact, for a ten-year-old, I would say she is gifted."

Cucu pinched Safiyah's cheek and laughed. "Gifted?" She studied the mural that swept like a scarf across the wall. "Oh, my." She clapped her hand to her chest. "That looks like…" She turned to Safiyah. "Our journey to the city? The road that went on forever?"

"I tell you what." Mr. Littlejohn's voice was brisk, as if he wanted to distract Cucu from sad memories. "The school can spare all the paste Safiyah needs. And with Pendo to help, I am sure her mural will be finished soon."

Cucu gave Safiyah a look of surprise.

Later she would tell her grandmother how she and Pendo were friends again, thought Safiyah. So easily, with just a few words.

"But will you allow me one thing?" Mr. Littlejohn asked Cucu. "I would like to send a photographer to take pictures of the house."

"Photos!" Pendo jumped up and down. "Can I be in them?"

"That will be up to the photographer," he said. "And Safiyah."

"Saffy? Please say I can," begged Pendo.

"First you have to promise," said Safiyah.

"Anything!"

"You have to put the pictures only where I tell you. It's my mural."

"I promise." Pendo linked arms with Safiyah.

"That's settled." Mr. Littlejohn took Cucu's arm and let her rest her weight on him as he led her back indoors.

Safiyah watched them go. She scuffed the ground with her foot. "I'm sorry I was mean to you, Pendo."

"And I'm sorry I wrecked your picture." The girls stood together for a moment, studying the mural. Then they sat on Cucu's bench swinging their legs until Pendo's feet were just as dirty as Safiyah's.

"Do you know how to play mancala?" asked Safiyah.

"Of course I do." Pendo's tiny braids bobbed as she nodded. "My father plays with the church deacon for hours and hours." She rolled her eyes. "While they talk about God."

"I thought only ladies played," said Safiyah. "Cucu taught me when we were at the clinic. Shall we play now?"

"I have to help Mr. Littlejohn find his way back to school first," Pendo told her as she stood up. "Then I will go home and change—"

"Those lovely clothes!" said Safiyah, sounding just like her grandmother.

Both girls laughed.

It was good to be friends again.

Chapter Nineteen

It took almost three weeks to finish the paper house. Safiyah and Pendo worked into the early evenings, while the neighborhood filled with the bustle of people on their way home from work. The smell of fires and cooking suppers wove through the alleyways, and stray dogs curled up in the shadows with their noses twitching.

The girls used two more jars of Mr. Littlejohn's paste. But Safiyah did not need to go back to the garbage dump to find more pictures.

One morning, a woman in a maid's uniform stopped to admire the mural. On her way home that night she gave Safiyah a plastic bag full of old magazines. "My boss never throws anything out. He said I could have these," she said. The man who collected cans often perched on his cart to watch them work. One day he brought a bundle of magazines tied up in string.

Sometimes people left so much paper on her bench that there was hardly room for Cucu to sit down.

During the day while Pendo was at school, Safiyah chose the pictures she wanted and cut them out. She moved them into piles, made new piles, then moved them again. Then she laid them out to figure out how to piece them together.

Each afternoon, Pendo came to help after she had changed out of her school uniform and finished her chores. But now she waited for Safiyah to tell her where to put the pictures before she helped paste up any of them.

At last all four walls were covered, even places so low down that they had to crawl along the dirty ground to reach them or so high they had to stand on the rickety chair.

That evening, Safiyah led her grandmother along the mural. Cucu was stronger now. She didn't need to lean on her stick as she stopped to look at her favorite pictures.

"Now come around again," said Safiyah. "But stand farther back. What do you see?" She held her breath as she waited. What if her grandmother couldn't see the stories she had tried to create? What if they were just in her own head, and all she had done was make a patchwork of pretty colors?

As they went round the second time, Cucu used her stick to point. "This is the long road we walked along after we left our home." She waved higher. "Here is our village." She leaned closer. "And the people whose faces we cannot see…" She spoke softly to herself. "These are the ones we left behind. Our friends, and others who are no longer with us… your mother, my only daughter, perhaps?"

Safiyah nodded silently as her grandmother gazed up at the place that was too far to reach, as they both thought of the people who were now part of their old life.

Cucu moved on until she came to a heap of mixed-up shapes and colors. "That is the garbage dump, I think. Where you spend so much time when you are not home with your old cucu."

Safiyah nodded, her eye on the gray clouds that hovered above it.

Cucu turned the corner of the house. "And here is our street." She giggled as she pointed at the wall. "The water vendor's stand here. And Mr. Zuma's bicycle shop, filled with all his bits and pieces!" She grasped Safiyah's arm as her gaze swept farther along. "The fire!" She stared at the flames of red and yellow that licked up the wall.

She led Safiyah quickly on, as if she wished to leave behind the fire, and its bad memories. "Ah. Here is the clinic," she said. "All those white walls. Weren't they wonderful. And what is that…?"

"It is called a stethoscope," said Safiyah. She had cut it from a page filled with shining medical instruments. "The doctor let me wear his when you were sick."

"And here we are home again," said Cucu. She didn't just mean her bench beside the doorway. She was looking at Safiyah's mural of their house as it once was, just broken boards and sheets of rusted metal. Before Safiyah made it into a home full of color and life. "Pendo's Mr. Littlejohn is right." Cucu pulled Safiyah close and stroked her hair. "Such a clever girl. Talented, as he said. And just as he said, you are indeed a gift."

Chapter Twenty

"But there's still lots more paper," Pendo said when Safiyah announced the next day that the paper house was all done. She flipped through the pages left in Rasul's box. "Mr. Littlejohn has lots more paste."

"It's finished, Pendo." Safiyah put her arm around her friend's shoulder.

"It was fun," said Pendo. "At first I when I saw all the mixed-up colors, I didn't know it was a design. But now it's like a story."

Kibera was a little like her mural, Safiyah thought. So much was mixed up and muddled and frightening if you looked closely. But from a distance, you could see the pattern to it. And every day that she lived here it made more sense and felt just a bit more like home.

Safiyah and Pendo picked up the leftover scraps of paper that fluttered around on the ground. As they worked, people stopped to look at the house, to talk to each other and to smile at Safiyah and Pendo.

Some asked questions. Others nodded and murmured as they looked at the long road that had led Cucu and Safiyah from their village. Some visitors told their own stories of coming to Kibera for work and a better life. They named people they had left behind and family members who had died or disappeared into the city since they arrived.

She and Cucu were not the only people who were a long way from home, Safiyah realized. There were so many people with similar stories.

When all the stray paper was cleared away, Pendo asked, "Shall I tell Mr. Littlejohn that the photographer can come now?"

Safiyah studied the house, wondering how it would look in a picture.

"Or you can come to school tomorrow and tell him yourself," offered Pendo.

"No. You do it," Safiyah said. Pendo had been the one to tell her about putting paper on walls. She was the one who had asked for the scissors and paste.

"And I can still be in the picture?" Pendo asked.

Safiyah hugged her. "It's your paper house too."

"It's everyone's, I guess," said Pendo. "So many people stop to look at it." She handed Safiyah the jar of paste. "Do you want to keep this?"

Safiyah took it from her. She made sure the lid was screwed on tight. She would keep it in the tin with the worn threads that were all that were left of the bracelet her mother had made her so long ago.

@

The photographer was a tall young man with a big camera around his neck. He carried a bulging brown bag over his shoulder.

"This is Mr. Amar Dhillon from the Kenyan News Service," said Mr. Littlejohn. Mr. Dhillon shook hands with Cucu. "My card, missus."

She frowned at the little piece of paper he gave her before she tucked it into her dress.

Pendo's teacher introduced the photographer to Safiyah and Pendo. Even to Chidi, who had shown up when he heard that someone would be taking pictures. Chidi was so excited, he couldn't stand still.

Mr. Dhillon arranged Safiyah, Pendo and Cucu in a little group. "Here. Stand here. No you, over here."

"I want to be in the picture," whined Chidi. Mr. Littlejohn put his hand on his shoulder to keep him still. But Chidi soon slipped away to peek into Mr. Dhillon's big bag.

Mr. Dhillon took photos of Safiyah by herself in the doorway looking out, and others as she stood looking at the house, first from the left, then from the right. He took pictures of Safiyah and Pendo with their arms around each others' shoulders. Then standing with their arms by their sides. He told them to smile, over and over again, until their cheeks hurt.

When he took pictures of Cucu on her bench, she smiled without needing to be told.

Meanwhile, Mr. Littlejohn strolled around the house. "Wonderful," he said. "Look at this!" He touched the fire mural. "And this lovely tree—it is a tree?—against the blue sky. Is this your village? Yes. I can see it." He studied the walls up close and looked at them again from a distance.

Chidi followed the teacher, copying every move, stroking his chin, nodding slowly. Everyone thought it was very funny, but Mr. Littlejohn didn't seem to notice.

Neighbors clustered around. Some tried to sneak into the pictures or gave Mr. Dhillon advice that he ignored. He tried to shoo the audience away, especially the neighborhood children who wanted to have their pictures taken too.

Safiyah and Pendo soon got bored, standing this way, then that. Cucu sent Chidi next door to play with the little boys who now lived in Mrs. Okella's house. "I'm going inside, away from this fuss," she said.

Mr. Dhillon kept taking photos. He balanced on the old chair and knelt in the dirt. He went around and around the shack taking pictures from all kinds of angles.

He took one group picture of everyone who wanted to be in it. Cucu stood in front holding hands with Safiyah on one side and Pendo on the other. The camera clicked and whirred.

At last Mr. Dhillon packed it back in his bag. He was done.

Everyone clapped. They patted Mr. Dhillon on the back and shook Mr. Littlejohn's hand. They shook hands with Pendo and Safiyah. The women hugged them and pinched their cheeks.

Before Mr. Dhillon left with Mr. Littlejohn, he gave Safiyah one of his little white cards. "It says his name. *Amar Singh Dhillon,*" said Pendo as she read over Safiyah's shoulder. "Then *Photographer, IFPO. RSP.* I wonder what those letters mean. Maybe he is famous."

"I didn't like him," said Safiyah. "Move here. Stand there. No, this way. Smile. Don't smile."

"Bossy, bossy, bossy," said Pendo.

"Bossy, bossy, bossy," echoed Safiyah.

They fell against each other giggling.

When they had both got their breath back, Pendo picked up her schoolbag and hung it over her shoulder. "I better go home. I didn't like Mr. Dhillon either, but I am glad you let me be in the pictures."

"Have you got homework?" asked Safiyah.

"I have twenty words to learn for a test tomorrow," Pendo told her.

Pendo had homework for school tomorrow. Cucu was indoors, resting from the excitement of the afternoon. As she watched her friend disappear around the corner at the end of the street, Safiyah slumped onto Cucu's bench.

Her mural was done. But nothing else had changed.

Chapter Twenty-One

It was hardly light when Safiyah was woken a few days later by a voices in the street. She peeked outside. "Cucu! Cucu wake up."

Her grandmother's face emerged from the blanket. Her hair stuck up like curled wire. "What is it, child?"

"People. Hundreds of them, outside."

Cucu sat up. "People are always stopping to look at your lovely house."

When Cucu and Safiyah stood in the doorway, they found the alley filled with people. Some going and some coming while others stood talking to each other, pointing at the paper house.

Pendo pushed through the crowd, holding a newspaper above her head. "Saffy. Your house is in the paper!"

"What do you mean, child?" Cucu pulled Pendo out of the scrum of people. "Away now," she cried. "Have you no work to go to? No families to tend to?"

A few people moved away. But many stayed as even more came down the alley.

"Mr. Dhillon's pictures," said Pendo. "Look!" She held up the newspaper for Cucu and Safiyah to see.

One wall of the paper house almost filled the front page. In another photograph, Cucu sat on her bench. She was smiling so hard that every one of her few teeth showed. Huge letters ran across the top page. "*Child Brings Color to Dark and Dangerous Place*," read Pendo. "That's what it says."

"Dangerous!" huffed Cucu. "How can my own home be dangerous?" She squinted at the picture.

Safiyah took the newspaper from Pendo. Cucu looked so proud and happy in the photo. Even in her frayed and faded dress.

"There are more photos inside," said Pendo. "On page seven."

They huddled around the newspaper to look at the pictures that filled two whole pages. One showed Cucu standing with her back to the camera as she pointed at the fire that blazed across the wall. Another was of

Safiyah and Pendo with their arms around each other. There was one of Pendo in her smart red and blue uniform, while next to her stood Safiyah in her old shorts and yellow T-shirt with the hole in the shoulder.

Safiyah felt her face flush with shame. Cucu looked like the proud old lady she was, the kind grandmother who Safiyah loved more than anyone in the world. While she looked like a poor little girl who couldn't even go to school. "Here. You can have it." She shoved the newspaper into Pendo's arms. "Hang it up for everyone to see, you in your lovely clothes. Show it to all your friends. But I don't want to look at it again."

"Safiyah!" cried Cucu as Safiyah ducked indoors away from the prying eyes and chattering voices. "What is wrong now? Our lovely house. Look! In the important newspaper for all to see."

Safiyah did not answer her grandmother. She threw herself on the bed and pulled the thin covers over her head to keep out the nosy world.

Chapter Twenty-Two

Safiyah stayed indoors all day. Just as Cucu had done when she was so sick.

All day she heard her grandmother telling passers-by why her granddaughter had started her mural. "To help make an old lady well," she said proudly. She led them around the house to point out the village they had come from. She described their long journey by bus and on foot and in a low voice told them how Safiyah's mother had died. Cucu described the fire that had killed Mrs. Okella. And explained that she had been in the clinic, but was better now.

Some people murmured sounds of sympathy and sadness. Others told their own stories, some stories just as sad as Safiyah and her grandmother's, others about new friends who helped them adjust to life in Kibera.

Between visitors, Safiyah heard the rustle of the newspaper as Cucu sat on her bench just outside the door, turning the pages again and again.

Late in the day when Cucu came indoors to light the lamp, she brought presents from the visitors. A plantain and a bottle of Coca Cola. "Here's a book for you," she said as she handed it to Safiyah. "We will ask Pendo to tell us what it is called. And look at this lovely bread. We will have it with our soup."

Safiyah turned her face to the wall. Her beautiful house was in the newspaper. But so was she. A girl with old clothes, who couldn't even read the words that told her what page to turn to see more pictures.

She was huddled under her blanket when the doorway curtain was pushed aside. "Are you sick now?"

Safiyah sat up. Rasul! Still sneaking up on her. "What do you want?" she asked.

"I came to pay homage to the great artist!" He bowed deeply. When he stood up again, he was grinning.

"Don't make fun of me," she said.

"I'm just repeating what everyone is saying."

"Who is everyone?" asked Cucu.

"The newspaper, for a start," said Rasul. "And your teacher, Mr. Littlejohn?"

"He's not my teacher."

"He will be soon." Rasul grinned again.

"Go away," Safiyah told him. She pulled her blanket higher.

"Saffy!" Cucu frowned at her.

The light shifted as Rasul stood in the doorway. "You sure you don't want to know more? You are to get what you have wanted all along."

A glimmer of an idea squirmed inside Safiyah. "What have I wanted all along?"

"To go to school. Like Pendo and chattering Chidi," said Rasul. "You're to get a scholarship."

Cucu grabbed Safiyah's hand and held it tight.

"Someone has offered to pay for Saffy to go to school," Rasul told her.

"For books?" Safiyah swung her feet over the edge of the bed. "For a uniform?"

Rasul nodded. "For everything. And you will get special lessons. At the art college."

Safiyah's heart thumped in her chest. She would go to school with Pendo. She would wear a red sweater and blue skirt.

She would learn to read!

"Who is paying for this scholarship?" asked Cucu.

"A rich geezer," Rasul told her, "who likes art."

"Why?" Cucu sounded as if she did not believe a word of it.

"He recognizes Safiyah's outstanding talent. Those were his words."

Cucu's hand shook on Safiyah's as she asked him, "How do you know all this?"

Rasul leaned against the doorway. "Mr. Littlejohn showed the newspaper to the teachers. They told all the kids in their classes, which is how Chidi heard all about it. The brat happened to be in school today, for a change. And on his way home he stole two copies off the newsstand, which is how we know all about it." He stuck his hands in the pockets of his bright yellow pants. "Ma is so happy for you, she can't stop smiling." His face was sad for a moment. Perhaps he was thinking of his sister who liked school so much, thought Safiyah. But then he winked at her. "It may be a while until Chidi smiles though," he said.

"Did you beat him for stealing?" asked Safiyah.

"He deserves it. But no one gets beaten in my house." He grinned. "He has to pay back the news vendor. So he's off now, collecting bottles at the dump, I bet."

That's where this all started, thought Safiyah. At the dump. Looking for paper so she could fix the house for her sick grandmother.

Rasul dug a rolled newspaper out of his pocket. "Here. I bought a copy for you."

"Cucu has one already," said Safiyah. "You know I can't read it."

"This is no time to sulk, little girl! You can look at the pictures, can't you?" said Rasul. "And maybe if you look at them long enough, you will believe what that art fellow has to say. 'Extraordinary talent. Keen observation. Great initiative.' And lots more." He pulled Safiyah her to her feet. "Pendo will read it to you. She's outside giving tours of the paper house."

Safiyah found her friend talking to two men at the side of the house. She was wearing her usual shorts and the old green sweater with a hole in the elbow. Pendo's school uniform was at home, keeping clean.

Without it, she and Safiyah did not look so different.

She would have a school uniform soon, just like Pendo, thought Safiyah. She would take it off after school and put it away carefully before she changed into her old familiar clothes. Clothes she had brought with her when they traveled the long road from the village.

She would go to art classes. Just like Rasul said. Like it said in the newspaper that she would keep in her special tin under the bed.

But what if she didn't want to be an artist?

Safiyah linked arms with Pendo and said, "I want to show you something." She led her friend to the picture of medical instruments. She pointed out the stethoscope and told Pendo how she might be a nurse instead of an artist, so she could help the sick people who crowded the beds and the floor and the courtyard of the clinic.

But first she would go to school. Where she would learn to read.

Safiyah and Pendo spent a long time looking at the newspaper pictures and studying every inch of the mural on the walls of the paper house.

Later, while Cucu heated soup on the little stove, they sat together outside and listened to the noises of Kibera swirling all around. They looked across the roofs at the birds chattering on the power lines.

Behind them, the house blazed with shapes and colors, telling the story of Safiyah's life here and back in her old home.

"Tell me again what it says in the paper," said Safiyah. She tipped her head against Pendo's shoulder as she imagined them walking together to school in matching red sweaters and blue skirts. She would learn to read and write like Pendo—and Chidi. She would grow up to be an artist or a nurse or even a doctor, so that one day she could earn enough money for a better house in the city. Or so that she and Cucu could return to their village to help the people left behind.

Until then, with friends and neighbors like Mrs. Pakua and Rasul—and even little pest Chidi—life here was not so bad. Safiyah closed her eyes as she listened to her best friend Pendo read words that one day she would be able to read herself, about their new life in Kibera and the paper house they were all so proud of.

A few facts about life in an African slum

Kibera is a slum on the outskirts of Nairobi, Kenya.

As many as half a million people may live there, most without running water, electricity or bathrooms.

Many have been forced to leave their villages by drought, which causes crop failure and starvation. They come to the city looking for work. But there is never enough work for everyone.

Many Kenyan children have lost at least one relative to AIDS. Many live with a grandparent, aunt or uncle and other family members. Tuberculosis and pneumonia are other serious diseases that affect people in the slums.

Not all children can afford to go to school. But many are helped with money donated by people in other countries.

Despite their poverty, the people of Kibera have schools, churches, clinics and community centers. Children play, neighbors get to know each other and people organize ways to help those most in need.

For many people, life in the slum may be the only one they will ever know. But those with a good education have the best chance of making a better life.

Mancala, one of the oldest games in the world, is played by adults and children all over Africa and in many other countries.

Ten percent of author royalties from the sale of *The Paper House* will be donated to Kibera's Red Rose School, Nairobi through The Children of Kibera Foundation at www.childrenofkibera.org.

Acknowledgments

No idea goes anywhere without the wonderful input from my husband Douglas Brunt. And my dream editor, Sarah Harvey, helps me get the story right. Then there are all my writing peers who cheer me on, and the readers who send me wonderful letters. Without them all, I would be writing in the dark.

Lois Peterson wrote short stories and articles for adults for twenty years before writing *Meeting Miss 405,* her first novel for children. Her next children's book was *The Ballad of Knuckles McGraw*, followed by *Silver Rain*. She was born in England, and has lived in Iraq, France and the United States. She now lives in Surrey, British Columbia, where she works in a public library, writes, reads and teaches creative writing to adults, teens and children.